CAUGHT STEALING

BY JAKE MADDOX

Text by Brandon Terrell
Illustrated by Aburtov

STONE ARCH BOOKS
a capstone imprint

Jake Maddox books are published by Stone Arch Books,
A Capstone Imprint
1710 Roe Crest Drive
North Mankato, Minnesota 56003
www.capstonepub.com

Library of Congress Cataloging-in-Publication Data
Maddox, Jake, author. Caught stealing / by Jake Maddox ; text by Brandon
Terrell ; illustrated by Aburtov.

 pages cm. -- (Jake Maddox sports stories)

Summary: When his father's valuable signed baseball disappears during
the team's sleepover, Ian Shin, catcher for the Scottsville Knights, suspects
the new pitcher, Hunter Yates, but he cannot be sure, and his trust in his
teammates is shattered — so he must uncover the truth to bring the team back
together.

ISBN 978-1-4965-0493-7 (library binding) -- ISBN 978-1-4965-0497-5 (pbk.) --
ISBN 978-1-4965-2325-9 (ebook pdf) -- 978-1-4965-2467-6 (reflowable epub)

1. Catchers (Baseball)--Juvenile fiction. 2. Baseball teams--Juvenile fiction. 3.
Theft--Juvenile fiction. 4. Trust--Juvenile fiction. 5. Teamwork (Sports)--
Juvenile fiction. [1. Baseball--Fiction. 2. Stealing--Fiction. 3. Trust--Fiction.
4. Teamwork (Sports)--Fiction.] I. Terrell, Brandon, 1978- author. II. Aburto,
Jesus, illustrator. III. Title. IV. Series: Maddox, Jake. Impact books. Jake
Maddox sports story.

PZ7.M25643Cau 2016
813.6--dc23
[Fic]

2014043707

Art Director: Bob Lentz
Graphic Designer: Veronica Scott
Production Specialist: Katy LaVigne

Printed in Canada
032015   008825FRF15

TABLE OF CONTENTS

CHAPTER 1
WALK-OFF 5

CHAPTER 2
SLUMBER PARTY..10

CHAPTER 3
MISSING!..18

CHAPTER 4
A THIEF AMONG THEM?...................................... 22

CHAPTER 5
DISTRACTED 28

CHAPTER 6
FALLING APART..35

CHAPTER 7
THE TRUTH UNCOVERED 40

CHAPTER 8
SORRY 46

CHAPTER 9
BACK ON TRACK..52

CHAPTER 10
TRUST YOUR FRIENDS..57

CHAPTER 1

WALK-OFF

"Strike two!" the umpire bellowed.

Ian Shin, catcher for the Scottsville Knights, threw the ball back to the pitcher. Then he adjusted his mask, squatted behind the plate, and smacked his fist into his mitt.

"Come on, Hunter!" Ian shouted.

Hunter Yates leaned forward on the mound. He rested his tattered glove on one knee and squinted at Ian. Ian pointed one finger toward the dirt, signaling for a fastball right down the middle.

It was the first game of the season, and while many of the Knights had played together last season, Hunter was new to the team. His family had just moved to Scottsville. He was quiet and didn't talk much with the other guys at practice. Ian didn't mind, though. Hunter was a great pitcher. He was tall, with broad shoulders and dark, piercing eyes. He wore his hat low to hide them, which made batters uneasy.

And he was a fastball machine.

Hunter reared back and fired the ball toward home plate. The batter for the opposing team — the Rochester Buzzards — leaped back as the pitch snapped into Ian's mitt so hard it stung his hand.

"Steee-rike three!" the umpire shouted, jerking his thumb toward the sky. "Yoouu're out!"

That was three outs. The crowd seated in the bleachers behind the backstop cheered as the Knights jogged off the field.

In the dugout, the team congratulated Hunter on his amazing pitching. Coach Frey, a man with long sideburns and a square chin, patted Hunter on the back and said, "Another great inning."

"Thanks, Coach," Hunter said quietly, taking his seat on the bench.

It was the bottom of the seventh — the final inning in the local sixth-grade baseball league — and the score was tied 1–1.

Ian was "in the hole," which meant he would be the third person up to bat. The team's first baseman and Ian's best friend, Willie Moyers, was up first.

"Let's win this game, guys!" Ian shouted.

Unlike Hunter, whose pitching had been strong throughout the game, the Buzzards' pitcher seemed tired. Willie jumped on the first pitch and hit a single into right field. The Knights whooped and hollered from their dugout.

The next batter was Matt, the Knights' speedy center fielder. He hit a grounder toward the third-base line. Willie raced to second as the Knights' pitcher scooped up the ball and threw Matt out at first.

Then Ian was up. He grabbed his bat and walked up to the plate, knocking the dirt from his cleats as he stepped into the batter's box.

One good hit, and I can win this game, Ian thought.

The first pitch was low. Ball one. The second was outside. Ball two. Ian's bat didn't leave his shoulder for either one. The third pitch, though, was just right.

Crack!

The second the bat connected with the ball, Ian knew the Buzzards' outfielders wouldn't catch it. The ball landed in a gap and bounced to the fence.

Willie ran home easily, where the whole team greeted him. Ian rounded the bases and raced over to join the celebration, completing an inside-the-park home run.

"We did it!" he shouted, high-fiving Willie.

The Knights had won!

CHAPTER 2

SLUMBER PARTY

"Who's hungry?" Ian's dad asked as he walked into the basement game room with a stack of steaming-hot, greasy pizza boxes in his arms later that night. "Pizza's here!" He set them on a table.

It was a tradition to have a slumber party at Ian's house after the first game of the season. Many of the kids were playing pool or throwing darts. Some were huddled in front of the television playing video games. But all of them turned when they heard the word pizza.

"Me! I'm hungry!" Ian's four-year-old brother Benny shouted, buzzing around the pizza boxes like a fly. "I like cheese pizza!"

"Get lost!" Ian said, waving his brother away as his teammates began grabbing slices of pizza.

His dad gave him a stern look.

"Sorry, Benny," Ian muttered.

"Can I hang out with you guys?" Benny asked eagerly.

Ian sighed. "Dad . . . ?"

"Come on, kiddo," Dad said, grabbing a paper plate and a couple slices of cheese pizza. "Let's go upstairs and watch a movie."

"Cool!" Benny shouted. Then he sprinted up the stairs.

The Knights wolfed down the pizzas in record time. As Ian was taking his turn playing a video game, he heard the doorbell ring upstairs.

Soon after, his dad came down the steps again. "Ian, looks like another Knight has arrived," he said.

Behind Ian's dad stood Hunter Yates.

Ian was beyond surprised. He hadn't thought Hunter would show up.

"Hey, man," Ian said, passing his game controller to Willie and standing up. "Come on in."

"Uh, thanks," Hunter said. He had a backpack slung over his shoulder.

Ian took it and set it behind the couch with the other players' belongings.

"There's soda in the fridge, and there are still some snacks. Have you played the new *Ninja Werewolves* game yet?" Ian asked.

Hunter shook his head. "What is it?" he asked.

Ian saw Willie's mouth drop open. "Dude, have you been living on Jupiter?" Willie asked. "*Ninja Werewolves* is, like, the most hyped game ever."

Hunter shrugged. "I don't really play video games," he said.

Everyone — Ian included — looked at Hunter as if he really had just arrived from Jupiter.

For the next hour or so, the Knights took turns fighting werewolves. Hunter just watched. He sat quietly behind the others, sipping his soda.

While Jackson, the team's shortstop, and Matt, the center fielder, were playing darts, Hunter stood nearby, gazing at an autographed, framed photo of Derek Jeter on the wall.

"Wait. Your dad has a signed Jeter?" Hunter asked.

"That's nothing," Jackson said. "Ian, you should show him your dad's office."

Ian led his teammates down the hall to his father's basement office. The room was filled with all sorts of sports memorabilia. The walls were covered in framed posters, and rows of shelves were filled with signed photos and trading cards. Ian loved browsing it all, but he knew not to touch anything.

The boys huddled in the room and gazed at the shrine to sports history.

"Whoa," Hunter whispered. He walked over and examined a baseball signed in blue ink and propped up inside a glass display case.

"That's my dad's prized possession," Ian explained. "It's a homerun ball hit and signed by Johnny Bench. He's my dad's favorite player. Mine too. He played catcher for the Cincinnati Reds, and now he's in the Hall of Fame."

Just then, a tiny voice from behind them said, "I don't think you guys should be in here."

Ian's heart leaped into his throat. He turned around and saw Benny standing in the doorway. "Leave us alone, pipsqueak!" Ian shouted. He lunged at Benny, who darted off down the hall, laughing.

"Hey, I brought my glow-in-the-dark football," Willie said. "Anyone want to go outside and play a little catch?"

"I do," Matt said.

"Sounds fun," Jackson added.

"Cool," Willie said. "Let's do it."

They filed out of the room and headed down the hall. Ian caught Hunter looking over his shoulder one more time before he followed as well.

Then Ian flicked off the light, closed the door, and headed outside to play football.

CHAPTER 3
MISSING!

The boys played football under the stars for over an hour. During the game, Hunter's cell phone rang, so he went inside to take the call.

When Hunter returned, he said, "That was my dad. I gotta go."

"Oh," Ian said. "Bummer."

Hunter nodded, then turned to go back inside to get his things. By the time the boys were finished playing football, Hunter's dad had picked him up.

The group tried their hardest to stay up all night, but one by one, each player rolled out his sleeping bag somewhere on the floor and dozed off. Ian and Willie were the last two awake. As they watched an old horror movie, Ian's eyelids slowly fluttered closed, and he drifted off to sleep.

He woke the next morning to the smell of bacon. His parents had cooked a massive breakfast for everyone. The team crowded around the dining room table and ate.

Afterward, a few of the guys who lived nearby walked home. The others waited for their parents to pick them up.

"See you at practice tomorrow," Willie said as he shouldered his backpack and sleeping bag and headed out the door to his mom's car.

When the house was empty, Dad said, "First things first, champ. Time to clean up that disaster zone downstairs, okay?"

"I'm on it," Ian said, grabbing a trash bag and heading to the basement. As he walked around checking for garbage, he noticed the door to his dad's office was wide open.

"Funny," he muttered. "I could've sworn I shut the door last night."

Ian walked down the hall and was about to close the door when he saw something. Or rather, when he didn't see something.

On the shelf in front of him was the glass display case that should have held his dad's most cherished piece of baseball history — the signed Johnny Bench baseball.

But the case was empty.

The ball was missing!

CHAPTER 4

A THIEF AMONG THEM?

"No way!" Willie's jaw dropped. "Stolen?"

Ian nodded.

"So what'd you do?" Willie asked.

"I found a baseball, faked a signature, and put it in the display case," Ian said. "I have to find that ball, though."

It was the following Monday night, and the two friends were walking together to the baseball field for their next game. Their parents had dropped them off and were looking for parking spots.

"Do you think one of the guys took it?" Willie asked.

"I don't know. Yeah," Ian said. "I mean, it would make sense. Right? We were all in Dad's room looking at his stuff."

"Who would steal from you?" Willie asked, lifting up his cap to scratch his head. "We're all friends."

Ian shrugged. He didn't have an answer.

Most of the team was already in the dugout when Ian and Willie arrived. Some played catch in the infield. Others ran warm-up laps around the field. The opposing team — the Hartford Crickets — was stretching near their dugout.

Ian set down the bulky bag that held his catcher's gear and watched his teammates, trying to see if anyone looked suspicious.

Could it be Matt? Ian wondered, watching the center fielder play catch in the outfield. *Or Jackson?* The shortstop was fielding grounders in the infield.

Ian didn't want to believe that someone on his team could betray his trust like that, but who else could have done it?

Finally, Coach Frey gathered the team in the dugout. "Great win the other night," he said. "Our fielding was fantastic, as was our pitching." Coach pointed at Hunter, who'd just arrived. He was sitting on the bench lacing up his cleats.

A couple of the guys nodded in agreement. Ian looked over at the quiet pitcher. That was when he saw the brand-new leather glove resting on the ground beside Hunter's feet.

Wait a second, Ian thought. He suddenly remembered how Hunter had been eyeing the signed baseball at the slumber party. How he'd gone inside while the others were playing football. How he'd left abruptly.

"No way," Ian whispered.

Sure, he didn't know the kid that well, but he knew that Hunter didn't have a lot of money. He lived in an older, slightly rundown part of town, and he'd been using an old, worn baseball glove that was probably a hand-me-down from a family member.

Maybe Hunter stole the baseball and sold it to get money for a new glove, Ian thought.

He watched as Hunter stood up, scooped his new leather glove off the ground, and bent it back and forth in his hands to loosen it up.

And before Ian could think about it anymore, Coach Frey shouted, "All right, boys! Let's play ball!"

CHAPTER 5
DISTRACTED

Because they were the home team, the Scottsville Knights took the field first.

Ian strapped on his leg guards and slid his chest plate over his head. Then he walked out to the field, crouched down behind the plate, and secured the mask over his face.

But Ian couldn't focus. His mind was reeling as he thought about Hunter stealing his dad's baseball and selling it at a pawnshop or something.

I'm never going to get the ball back, Ian thought. He stared out at the mound. Hunter stood there, playfully smacking a ball into his new glove.

Hunter wound up and sent the ball over the plate. His first practice pitch bounced off Ian's mitt and skittered away.

"Sorry!" Ian called, chasing down the ball. He shook his head, trying to clear it.

Moments later, the game started. The first batter for the Crickets stepped into the batter's box. The first pitch was a smoking fastball. The batter swung and missed. On the second pitch, he made contact. The ball dribbled just a few feet off the plate.

Ian leaped to his feet. He grabbed the ball and threw it to first. But his throw was high, and it sailed over Willie's head.

The batter easily advanced to second.

"That's all right!" Coach Frey shouted. "Shake it off, Ian."

Ian couldn't, though. The next batter connected for a hit to right field, and the base runner dashed for home. The throw to home plate was spot-on, but Ian let it bounce away from him.

The Crickets took an early 1–0 lead.

It was almost like Hunter could sense that Ian was distracted. His pitching over the next few innings was wild. By the end of the fourth inning, the Crickets were leading 4–0.

In the bottom of the fourth, Ian was the second person up to bat. He shed his catcher's gear, grabbed a bat and helmet, and stepped into the on-deck circle. The dugout was silent.

Matt was the first batter. The speedster sent the first pitch down the right field line for a stand-up triple.

That woke up the dugout and the crowd, who cheered and clapped.

"Way to rip it, Matt!" Willie shouted.

Ian stepped up to the plate next. He'd already struck out once, back in the first inning. He needed a good on-base hit to redeem himself.

The first pitch was high, but Ian swung anyway. His hit sailed over the backstop behind him.

"Foul ball!" the umpire shouted.

The second pitch caught the corner of the plate.

"Strike two!"

Ian could feel the frustration in his gut. He never struck out. He was a great hitter. How could he possibly — *smack!*

The pitcher sent a fastball down the heart of the plate.

"Strike three! You're out!"

Ian slunk back to the dugout. He threw his bat and helmet down in anger.

"Are you okay?" Willie asked.

Ian shook his head. "I think Hunter stole my dad's baseball," he said quietly. "I can't stop thinking about it."

"What do you mean?" Willie asked.

"I think he stole it, sold it, and bought his new glove with the money," Ian explained. "Remember how he went back inside? He had the opportunity."

"What about my new glove?" Hunter asked. He stood nearby, his hands clenched into fists at his side.

Oh no, Ian thought. *He heard me.*

"Dude, did you take Ian's dad's baseball the other night?" Willie asked abruptly.

"What?" Hunter said, shocked. "I didn't take anything."

"Then how could you afford such a nice glove?" Ian asked.

Hunter didn't answer. His jaw tightened, and his cheeks burned red. He stomped toward Ian and shoved him with both hands, right in the chest.

Ian stumbled backward, tripped over the bench, and fell onto his back in the dirt.

CHAPTER 6
FALLING APART

Ian was dazed. The wind had been knocked out of him, and he was trying hard to catch his breath.

"Hey! What's going on?" Coach Frey hollered as Hunter leaped over the bench and jumped on top of Ian.

The Knights gathered in a big circle around Ian and Hunter. Ian squirmed, trying to pull himself free of Hunter.

Soon Coach Frey was pulling Hunter away, and Ian scrambled to his feet.

"What is going on, you two?" Coach Frey demanded. He stood between the boys and looked back and forth at them, but neither spoke.

"Ian thinks Hunter stole something from his house the other night," Willie said. "Something valuable."

"I didn't steal anything," Hunter insisted.

"Then where'd you get that glove?" Willie asked.

"None of your business," Hunter snapped, taking a step toward Willie.

"Just relax," Coach said. "We've got a game to focus on. You can deal with this after, all right?"

"Yeah, okay," Ian muttered. He brushed the dust off his uniform, embarrassed.

"Everything okay, Coach?" the umpire asked, ducking his head into the dugout.

"Yeah, we're good." Coach Frey said.

They weren't, though. After the fight, Ian and Hunter couldn't get into a rhythm. Hunter refused to throw any of the pitches Ian asked for. Instead, he threw pitches that Ian had to chase. Many of them skittered to the backstop.

In the fifth inning, after the Crickets had scored four more runs, Coach Frey pulled Hunter from the game. Jesse, one of the team's relief pitchers, took over the mound, and Hunter sat quietly on the bench.

The Knights were able to score two runs in the sixth inning off a pair of doubles by Willie and Jackson and a base hit by the team's second baseman, Wyatt.

Ian, however, struck out again. It was the worst game he'd ever played.

The final score was Crickets 10, Knights 2.

After the game, the team silently gathered their things. As he left the dugout and went to meet his family by the bleachers, Ian was silent. Benny played on the bleachers, laughing.

"Rough game, champ," Dad said, squeezing him gently on the shoulder. Then he noticed the look on Ian's face and added, "Are you all right?"

"I'm fine," Ian said.

But that was far from the truth.

CHAPTER 7

THE TRUTH UNCOVERED

At school the next day, Ian did his best to avoid Hunter. He was still beyond angry with Hunter for stealing his dad's signed baseball just so he could buy a stupid new glove.

To make matters worse, Ian wasn't even sure he wanted to be a Knight anymore. He was embarrassed by the way he'd played and by the scuffle he'd had with Hunter. He'd never been in a fight before. And this was with another player. They were supposed to be a team.

As Ian gathered his things from his locker after school, Willie came over. "Practice should be interesting today," he said. "Coach Frey isn't going to go easy on us after the game last night."

"I'm not feeling so good," Ian said. "I think I'm getting sick. Tell Coach sorry, but I'm gonna head home."

Willie shot him a look. "Oh. Is this because of Hunter?" he asked.

Ian crammed his schoolbooks into his backpack and closed his locker. "Dude, I feel like I'm going to hurl," he said. "It's probably from the mystery-meat lasagna we ate at lunch."

"All right, man," Willie said. "Feel better."

"Thanks," Ian said, heading outside.

Ian was old enough to have a key to his house, and his parents trusted him enough to let him stay home alone for an hour or so after school. So when he got home, he sat in his room with his headphones on, listening to music and doing homework.

An hour later, his bedroom door burst open, and Benny came rocketing in. He leaped onto the bed next to Ian and yanked the headphones from his big brother's ears.

"Why are you home?" Benny asked.

Then Mom appeared in the doorway. "Don't you have practice, Ian?" she asked.

"My stomach hurts," Ian lied. "I came home to rest."

"I'll bring you some crackers," Mom said. "Maybe you should take a break from doing homework."

After his mom left the room, Ian put down his notebook. He decided to lie down for a bit and play with his handheld video game. Normally, he kept it on the table next to his bed. But today, it wasn't there.

Ian walked downstairs to find Mom and Dad making dinner and Benny coloring at the dining room table. "Has anyone seen my handheld game?" he asked.

"Hmm . . ." Mom responded. "Benny, weren't you playing with that earlier?"

Benny nodded. "I was squishing monsters on it," he said proudly.

"Next time ask before you take my stuff," Ian said. He trudged back upstairs and into Benny's messy room. Posters of cartoon characters covered the walls. Stuffed animals and racecars were strewn everywhere.

Ian looked all over for his game system, but he couldn't find it. He checked under blankets and on the floor. Finally, he picked up Benny's pillow and looked underneath it.

Nothing.

But the pillow was heavier than Ian had expected. Something was stuffed in the pillowcase.

Got it, Ian thought, reaching in to pluck out the game system.

What he found, though, wasn't his game.

The item was round. It had stitches.

Ian grabbed it and pulled it out of the pillowcase.

In his hand was the signed Johnny Bench baseball!

CHAPTER 8

SORRY

"Benny!" Ian shouted furiously.

He couldn't believe it. *Hunter didn't take Dad's baseball after all!* Ian thought. *It hadn't even left the house! I'm a terrible teammate for not trusting him.*

There were quick footsteps on the stairs, and then Benny was standing in the doorway. "Yeah?" his little brother said.

Ian held out the baseball. "Did you take this the other night when my team was here?" he demanded, even though he already knew the answer.

Benny stared down at the floor, looking guilty. "You said it was Dad's most favorite thing," he said. "I just wanted to have it for a little while."

Just then, Dad appeared behind Benny, a puzzled look on his face. "What's going on, boys?" he asked. Then he saw what Ian was holding. "Why is that out of my office?"

"Benny took it," Ian said. "And I thought one of my friends stole it from you."

"Did you accuse him of stealing it?" Dad asked.

Ian nodded.

His dad held out his palm, and Ian placed the baseball in it. "Then I think you know what you have to do, Ian," Dad said.

Another nod. "I feel awful. Could I have a ride over there now?" Ian asked.

* * *

Hunter and his family lived across town, on a road lined with one-story houses and trailers. As they drove, Ian looked for the right house, consulting the team roster which listed all the players' addresses. He and Dad found it at the end of the street.

Dad parked, and Ian got out of the car and walked up the cracked driveway. He climbed the steps and knocked on the door.

A woman with straight dark hair answered.

"Hi, is . . . uh, is Hunter home?" Ian asked.

"One minute," the woman said. She disappeared back into the house. Ian heard her say, "A friend is here to see you."

Hunter responded with, "Friend?"

A moment later, Hunter appeared in the doorway. When he saw Ian waiting on the porch, he rolled his eyes.

"What are you doing here?" Hunter asked. "I told you, I don't have your stupid baseball."

"I know," Ian said. He shoved his hands into his coat pockets. "I came to apologize."

"Oh," said Hunter.

"I'm sorry I thought you stole my dad's baseball. I should have trusted you," Ian said. "My brother was actually the one who took it."

Hunter smiled, just a little. Ian was pretty sure he'd never seen Hunter do that before.

"I'm sorry, Hunter," Ian said.

Hunter nodded. "Sorry I got angry and shoved you," he said.

He paused, picking at a splinter of wood on the doorframe. Then he said, "Honestly, I was more embarrassed than angry. I got the glove from one of those 'Toys for Kids' charities. My family doesn't have a lot of money. And I, uh . . . I don't have a lot of friends."

Ian smiled. "What are you talking about?" he asked. "You've got a whole team of them."

Hunter smiled back. "Sometimes it feels like I'm the odd one out, since you guys have been playing together for so long. But I'd like to get to know you all better." Then he paused for a moment before asking, "Hey, do you wanna come inside for a little bit and hang out?"

"Absolutely," Ian said.

CHAPTER 9

BACK ON TRACK

Before their game that week, Ian decided to come clean with his team about the missing baseball. "It was my fault for accusing Hunter when I should have trusted him," Ian explained. "We're friends again, though, and we're ready to kick some butt!" He and Hunter grinned at one another.

"Thanks for sharing, Ian. I'm glad you two have worked it out," Coach Frey said, smiling. Then to the rest of the team he added, "All right, Knights! Are we ready to win this game? Let's bring it in!"

The team huddled up, piled their hands in a circle, and cheered, "Goooooo Knights!"

Their game that night was in the nearby town of Fenton. The Fenton Owls were the best team in the league, and they were going to be hard to beat. Their starting pitcher, a kid named Luke Miller, was just as good — if not better — than Hunter.

The Knights batted first. Willie was the leadoff man. He stepped up to the plate and watched as the first pitch sizzled past him.

"Strike!" the umpire bellowed.

Ian saw Willie's eyes grow large. The pitches were fast. Willie fouled the second pitch off, then swung and missed at the next — a strikeout.

The next batter grounded out to the shortstop, and the next hit a pop fly.

Ian strapped on his catcher's gear as the Knights took the field. Hunter stepped onto the mound and paced around anxiously.

The leadoff batter for the Owls toed the dirt, took a few practice swings, and stepped into the box.

Hunter wound up and threw harder and faster than Ian had ever seen. The ball sailed past the batter so fast he didn't even have time to swing. Strike one!

"Great pitching!" Coach Frey shouted from the dugout.

The game ended up being a true pitcher's duel. Neither team was able to get a runner past first base until the bottom of the fifth inning, when the Owls strung three hits together and loaded the bases.

Luke Miller stepped to the plate.

"You've got this guy!" Ian shouted to Hunter. He heard Luke snort at his comment.

Hunter leaned forward, read the sign — an inside fastball, hard to hit solidly — and pitched.

Luke Miller swung and smashed it high and far. Ian's heart leaped into his throat. *Stay in the park,* he wished.

It did, but just barely. The ball knocked off the wall in center field, and the bases cleared.

And just like that, the Owls led 3–0.

CHAPTER 10

TRUST YOUR FRIENDS

"Don't give up yet, boys," Coach Frey said as he paced in the dugout. He spit sunflower seeds into the dirt.

It was the top of the sixth, and the Knights only had two chances left to tie or win the game.

The Owls put in a relief pitcher with a fresh arm, but the new pitcher had a hard time finding the strike zone. After two walks in a row, Willie belted a double into left field, bringing both base runners across the plate and cutting the Owls' lead to 3–2.

"Great hit!" Ian cheered.

Next up was Matt. He hit a single and then proceeded to steal second base.

After two of his teammates struck out, it was Ian's turn to step up to the plate. He watched the first pitch as it sailed high. The second pitch was a change-up that floated right over the heart of the plate.

Ian swung with all his might. Bat and ball connected, and the ball soared deep into left field.

Ian ran hard, rounding first and heading for second. Ahead of him, Matt touched home for the tying run. Ian ran to third, and as he did, the relay throw went flying over the third baseman's head.

"Score! Score!" the team chanted from the dugout.

Ian ran down the line, legs pumping. He slid feet first just as the third baseman snatched up the ball and fired it to the catcher.

"Safe!" the umpire shouted. The dugout and bleachers erupted in cheers.

At the end of the inning, the Knights had the lead, 4–3.

"Bottom of the seventh," Ian said as he and Hunter walked out of the dugout together. "Three outs away from a win."

"Yeah. No pressure or anything," Hunter said, smiling. He and Ian slapped gloves, then split up and took their positions.

Hunter's fastball still had some zing to it, and the first batter hit a shallow fly ball to center field. Matt dashed in and plucked it out of the air easily.

"One out!" Ian shouted. "Keep it up!"

The next batter watched a couple of outside pitches, then turned on one and hit a solid single into left field.

The batter after him hit a hard grounder to Jackson. He dove, gloved the ball, and popped up, throwing a bullet to first base. Willie stretched out and scooped up the ball just before it hit the dirt.

"Two down!" Ian hollered.

The Knights were one out away from victory when Luke Miller stepped up to the plate.

"Time!" Ian shouted. He stood and jogged to the mound.

Hunter looked worried. "I haven't struck this guy out all night," he said.

"You've got a killer fastball, dude. Use it," Ian said.

"How do you know it'll work?" Hunter asked.

Ian smiled. "Because I trust you."

Ian walked back to home plate as the umpire yelled, "Play ball!" He took his position and dropped one finger to the dirt.

Hunter threw a fastball down the plate. Luke Miller reared back and unleashed a crushing swing.

The ball flew high into the air — so high it looked like it would scrape the clouds.

But it didn't go far. It was an infield pop fly. Miller took off running anyway.

"Got it!" Hunter shouted. He waved off the other infielders.

Seconds later, the ball dropped down to earth like a meteor. It landed with a perfect *thwack* right in Hunter's brand-new leather glove. Halfway to first, Luke Miller stopped and shook his head with frustration.

"That's the game!" the umpire shouted. He could barely be heard over the roar of the cheering crowd. "Knights win!"

Ian rushed the mound, picking Hunter up off the ground in celebration. In seconds, the rest of the Knights surrounded the two boys. Everyone was jumping up and down and cheering.

Ian smiled, happy to have his team back together again. *This is what teamwork is all about,* he thought as he walked off the field surrounded by his teammates.

AUTHOR BIO

Brandon Terrell is the author of numerous children's books, including several volumes in both the Tony Hawk 900 Revolution series and the Tony Hawk Live 2 Skate series, graphic novels for Sports Illustrated Kids, chapter books, and a picture book about trains. When not hunched over his laptop writing, Brandon enjoys watching movies and television, reading, watching (and playing!) baseball, and spending time with his wife and two children in Minnesota.

ILLUSTRATOR BIO

Aburtov has worked as a colorist for Marvel, DC, IDW, and Dark Horse and as an illustrator for Stone Arch Books. He lives in Monterrey, Mexico, with his lovely wife, Alba, and his crazy children, Ilka, Mila, and Aleph.

GLOSSARY

adjusted (uh-JUHSS-tid) — moved or changed something slightly

betray (bee-TRAY) — to be disloyal to someone or something

cherished (CHER-isht) — valued or appreciated

frustration (fruhss-TRAY-shuhn) — the feeling of being unable to get something done

memorabilia (mem-ur-uh-BEEL-ee-uh) — objects someone collects to remember a certain person, place, or thing

possession (puh-ZESH-uhn) — something that belongs to you

redeem (ri-DEEM) — to save, or to make up for

signature (SIG-nuh-chur) — a person's name, written in his or her own unique way

tattered (TAT-urd) — old and torn

uneasy (uhn-EE-zee) — worried or uncomfortable

wolfed (WULFT) — ate quickly

DISCUSSION QUESTIONS

1. Ian accused Hunter of stealing his dad's treasured baseball. Could Ian have handled the situation in a better way? Talk about the possibilities.

2. Why do you think Ian was so quick to accuse Hunter? Discuss some possible reasons.

3. Do you think Hunter was right to shove Ian when he was confronted? Talk about why or why not.

WRITING PROMPTS

1. The signed Johnny Bench baseball is one of Mr. Shin's prized possessions. What is your most prized possession? Write a paragraph about why the item is important to you.

2. Willie stands up for Ian when he and Hunter start arguing about the baseball. Do you think he was right to stand up for his friend, even though he didn't know if Hunter was guilty? Write about your opinion.

3. Imagine that Ian had never apologized to Hunter. Write a different ending to this story.

BASEBALL DICTIONARY

- **diamond** — a baseball infield

- **double** — a hit that allows the batter to safely reach second base

- **double play** — a play in which two players are called out

- **dugout** — a shelter with a bench that faces a baseball field; the team and coaches sit here during the game

- **error** — the act of a fielder misplaying the ball, allowing runners to move up one or more bases

- **fly ball** — a baseball that is hit high into the air

- **foul ball** — a baseball batted into foul territory

- **grand slam** — a home run that is hit with three runners on base; all runners, including the batter, score

- **home run** — a hit that allows the batter to go around all the bases and score a run

- **mound** — a raised area of the infield on which the pitcher stands

- **no-hitter** — a baseball game in which a pitcher doesn't allow the opposing team any hits

- **single** — a hit that allows the batter to safely reach first base

- **triple** — a hit that allows the batter to safely reach third base

- **umpire** — a person who controls play and makes sure players are following the rules of the game

- **wild pitch** — a pitch that can't be caught by the catcher and allows a runner to move up a base

4 NEW BOOKS!

- **TOUCHDOWN TRIUMPH**
- **HOOP HUSTLE**
- **CAUGHT STEALING**
- **SOCCER SHAKE-UP**